SEEN ART?

THE MUSEUM OF MODERN ART, NEW YORK

VIKING

JON SCIESZKA AND LANE SMITH

TO EVERYONE LOOKING FOR ART —J. S. AND L. S.

VIKING
Published by Penguin Group
Penguin Young Readers Group, 345 Hudson Street, New York, New York 10014, U.S.A.

Penguin Books Ltd, Registered Offices: 80 Strand, London WC2R 0RL, England

First published in 2005 by Viking, a division of Penguin Young Readers Group,
and the Museum of Modern Art

10 9 8 7 6 5 4 3 2

Library of Congress Cataloging-in-Publication Data is available

ISBN 0-670-05986-2

Printed in U.S.A.
Set in Optima

Many of the artworks in this book are covered by claims for copyright cited
in the captions on pp. 45–48. All photographs by the Department of Imaging
Services, The Museum of Modern Art, New York, except for the photograph
of Alvar Aalto's Paimio Chair, which is by James Welling.

DESIGNED BY MOLLY LEACH

It all started when I told my friend Art I would
meet him on the corner of Fifth and Fifty-third.

I didn't see him. So I asked a lady walking up the avenue,

"Have you seen Art?"

"MoMA?" asked the lady.

"Uh . . . no, he's just a friend."

"Just down Fifty-third Street here. In that beautiful new building. You can't miss it."

She was right.
It was a brand-new building. I couldn't miss it.

But I didn't see Art. I did see an official-looking guy with a badge.

"You seen Art?" I asked.

"MoMA?" said the guy.

I figured this must be a secret code word.

"Yes."

"Your timing is perfect. We're just opening."
The badge guy opened the door for me.

I was in.

"How do you like our new look?" asked a lady just inside.

"Nice," I said. "I'm here for Art."

She smiled and nodded.

"MoMA," I added.

"Right this way," she said. And she took me up the stairs.

"There.

"Exactly," said a little man

I mean isn't it just everything?

Can't you just feel the restlessness?
The color?
The emotion?"

"Yeah, I see what you mean.
Very intense.
But I'm looking for Art."

behind me. He took me by the elbow to another room.

"Spreading joy around by color. The artist said it himself.
Look at that red!
Look at that open box of crayons
inviting us in.
The grandfather clock?
It has no hands.
Time is suspended."

"I see that. No kidding. That is a lot of red. But . . . is Art here?"

"Just what I was thinking," said a girl across the room. "Come with me. I'll show you art."

"Good," I said. "I was starting
to think I was in the wrong place."

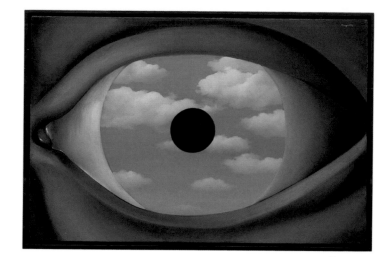

"Oh no," said the girl.
"You are in the right place. You just have to look. You have to see."

"Wow. I—"

"Yes," she said. "Your eye. Your dream can be what is real."

"What's with the ants attacking the gold watch?

And time is messed up here, too.

But where is Art?"

"You said it, brother."

A painter put his arm around me.

"Is it trying to **capture dreams?** Or is it making images everyone can recognize?

Look at those shapes. Are they letters of the alphabet?

Are they something more?"

"I guess they could be both," I said.
"But I'm just
looking for Art."

"This way," said a lady.
"I will take you to art."

"It's so . . . me."

It seemed like
everyone wanted
to help me find Art.

"The pain!
The mystery!"

"What composition."

"Look at the
constellations of shapes."

"The sense
of color is
remarkable,
don't you think?"

"So bold
and direct."

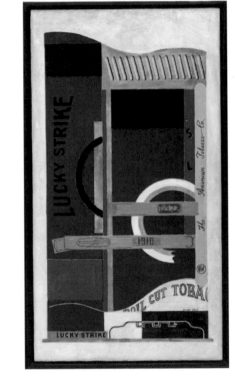

"Great atmosphere."

"I would answer, 'Not exactly the Art I was looking for.'"

'But is it art?'"

"The Bell-47D1 helicopter.

It weighs one thousand three hundred and eighty pounds.

It has a maximum airspeed of ninety-two miles per hour.

It was designed by a man who was also a painter and a poet.

A piece of delicate yet hard-working beauty.

Some might ask,

"Provocative."

"Powerful."

"So you see,
art is not just paintings."

"That's what I've
been trying to tell
everyone. Art is—"

"Yes, art is photos, video,
film, drawing, sculpture,
architecture . . ."

I decided to look for Art on my own.

"Whew."

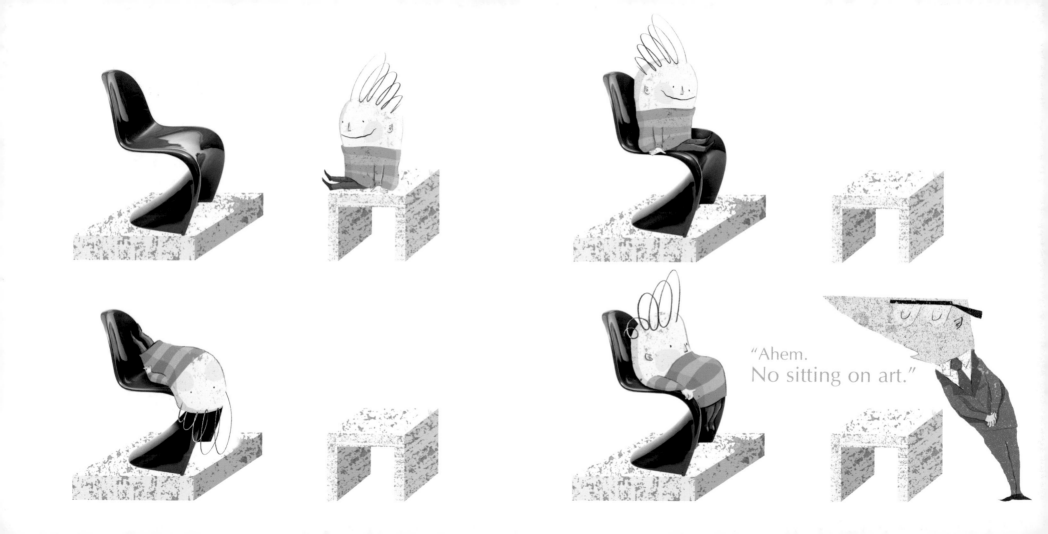

"Ahem.
No sitting on art."

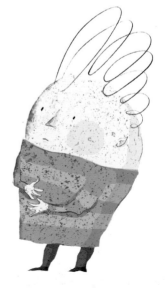

I had to find Art.

I looked in the garden.

The family there wasn't much help.

Neither was their goat.

I was starting to think I would never find Art.

I was beat, and right back where I started.

"Hello again.

Did you find art?"

Well, I thought . . .

I walked out of The Museum of Modern—

"Art. There you are."

"Of course," said Art.

"MoMA?" asked a man passing by.

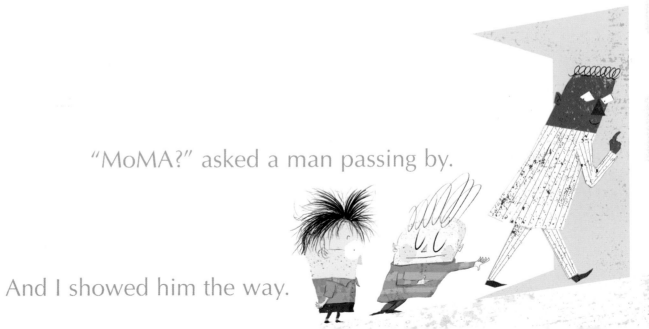

And I showed him the way.

ALL ABOUT THE ART

In dimensions, height precedes width precedes depth.

ALEXANDER CALDER
Lobster Trap and Fish Tail

1939. Hanging mobile: painted steel wire and sheet aluminum, 8′ 6″ (260 cm) x 9′ 6″ (290 cm) in diameter. Commissioned by the Advisory Committee for the stairwell of the Museum. The Museum of Modern Art, New York. © 2005 Estate of Alexander Calder/Artists Rights Society (ARS), New York

VINCENT VAN GOGH
The Starry Night

1889. Oil on canvas, 29 x 36¼″ (73.7 x 92.1 cm). The Museum of Modern Art, New York. Acquired through the Lillie P. Bliss Bequest

ALEXANDER CALDER
Black Widow

1959. Standing stabile: painted sheet steel, 7′ 8″ x 14′ 3″ x 7′ 5″ (233.3 x 434.1 x 226.2 cm). The Museum of Modern Art, New York. Mrs. Simon Guggenheim Fund. © 2005 Estate of Alexander Calder/Artists Rights Society (ARS), New York

ANDY WARHOL
Gold Marilyn Monroe

1962. Silkscreen ink on synthetic polymer paint on canvas, 6′ 11¼″ x 57″ (211.4 x 144.7 cm). The Museum of Modern Art, New York. Gift of Philip Johnson. © 2005 Andy Warhol Foundation for the Visual Arts/Artists Rights Society (ARS), New York

ANDY WARHOL
Before and After

1961. Synthetic polymer paint on canvas, 54 x 69⅞″ (137.2 x 177.5 cm). The Museum of Modern Art, New York. Gift of David Geffen. © 2005 Andy Warhol Foundation for the Visual Arts/Artists Rights Society (ARS), New York

EDWARD RUSCHA
OOF

1962 (reworked 1963). Oil on canvas, 71½ x 67″ (181.5 x 170.2 cm). The Museum of Modern Art, New York. © 2005 Edward Ruscha

ROY LICHTENSTEIN
Girl with Ball

1961. Oil and synthetic polymer paint on canvas, 60¼ x 36¼″ (153 x 91.9 cm). The Museum of Modern Art, New York. Gift of Philip Johnson. © 2005 Roy Lichtenstein

ROBERT RAUSCHENBERG
Bed

1955. Combine painting: oil and pencil on pillow, quilt, and sheet on wood supports, 6′ 3¼″ x 31½″ x 8″ (191.1 x 80 x 20.3 cm). The Museum of Modern Art, New York. Gift of Leo Castelli in honor of Alfred H. Barr, Jr. © 2005 Robert Rauschenberg

HENRI MATISSE
The Red Studio

1911. Oil on canvas, 71¼″ x 7′ 2¼″ (181 x 219.1 cm). The Museum of Modern Art, New York. Mrs. Simon Guggenheim Fund. © 2005 Succession H. Matisse, Paris/Artists Rights Society (ARS), New York

ALBERTO GIACOMETTI
Man Pointing

1947. Bronze, 70½ x 40¾ x 16⅜″ (179 x 103.4 x 41.5 cm). The Museum of Modern Art, New York. Gift of Blanchette Hooker Rockefeller. © 2005 Artists Rights Society (ARS), New York/ADAGP, Paris

MERET OPPENHEIM
Object
[Le Déjeuner en fourrure]

1936. Fur-covered cup, saucer, and spoon. Cup: 4⅜″ (10.9 cm) in diameter; saucer: 9⅜″ (23.7 cm) in diameter; spoon: 8″ (20.2 cm) long; overall height 2⅞″ (7.3 cm). The Museum of Modern Art, New York. Purchase. © 2005 Artists Rights Society (ARS), New York/Pro Litteris, Zurich

RENÉ MAGRITTE
The False Mirror

1928. Oil on canvas, 21¼ x 31⅞″ (54 x 80.9 cm). The Museum of Modern Art, New York. Purchase. © 2005 C. Herscovici, Brussels/Artists Rights Society (ARS), New York

SALVADOR DALÍ
The Persistence of Memory

1931. Oil on canvas, 9½ x 13″ (24.1 x 33 cm). The Museum of Modern Art, New York. Given anonymously. © 2005 Salvador Dalí, Gala-Salvador Dalí Foundation/Artists Rights Society (ARS), New York

BRADLEY WALKER TOMLIN
Number 20

1949. Oil on canvas, 7′ 2″ x 6′ 8¼″ (218.5 x 203.9 cm). The Museum of Modern Art, New York. Gift of Philip Johnson

WILLEM DE KOONING
Woman, I

1950–52. Oil on canvas, 6′ 3⅞″ x 58″ (192.7 x 147.3 cm). The Museum of Modern Art, New York. Purchase. © 2005 The Willem de Kooning Foundation/Artists Rights Society (ARS), New York

JEAN DUBUFFET
The Cow with the Subtle Nose

1954. Oil and enamel on canvas, 35 x 45¾″ (88.9 x 116.1 cm). The Museum of Modern Art, New York. Benjamin Scharps and David Scharps Fund. © 2005 Artists Rights Society (ARS), New York/ADAGP, Paris

JOAN MIRÓ
The Beautiful Bird Revealing the Unknown to a Pair of Lovers

From the Constellation series. 1941. Gouache, oil wash, and charcoal on paper, 18 x 15″ (45.7 x 38.1 cm). The Museum of Modern Art, New York. Acquired through the Lillie P. Bliss Bequest. © 2005 Successió Miró/Artists Rights Society (ARS), New York/ADAGP, Paris

ÉDOUARD VUILLARD
Interior, Mother and Sister of the Artist
1893. Oil on canvas, 18 1/4 x 22 1/4" (46.3 x 56.5 cm). The Museum of Modern Art, New York. Gift of Mrs. Saidie A. May. © 2005 Artists Rights Society (ARS), New York/ADAGP, Paris

EDVARD MUNCH
The Storm
1893. Oil on canvas, 36 1/8 x 51 1/2" (91.8 x 130.8 cm). The Museum of Modern Art, New York. Gift of Mr. and Mrs. H. Irgens Larsen and acquired through the Lillie P. Bliss and Abby Aldrich Rockefeller Funds. © 2005 The Munch Museum/The Munch-Ellingsen Group/Artists Rights Society (ARS), New York

EDWARD HOPPER
New York Movie
1939. Oil on canvas, 32 1/4 x 40 1/8" (81.9 x 101.9 cm). The Museum of Modern Art, New York. Given anonymously

MILTON AVERY
Sea Grasses and Blue Sea
1958. Oil on canvas, 60 1/8" x 6' 3/8" (152.7 x 183.7 cm). The Museum of Modern Art, New York. Gift of friends of the artist. © 2005 Milton Avery Trust/Artists Rights Society (ARS), New York

STUART DAVIS
Lucky Strike
1921. Oil on canvas, 33 1/4 x 18" (84.5 x 45.7 cm). The Museum of Modern Art, New York. Gift of The American Tobacco Company, Inc.

**ARTHUR YOUNG
BELL HELICOPTER INC., BUFFALO, N.Y.**
Bell-47D1 Helicopter
1945. Aluminum, steel, and acrylic plastic, 9' 2 3/4" x 9' 11" x 42' 8 3/4" (281.3 x 302 x 1271.9 cm). The Museum of Modern Art, New York. Marshall Cogan Purchase Fund

BILL TRAYLOR
Arched Drinker
c. 1939–42. Watercolor and pencil on cardboard, 14 x 13 3/4" (35.6 x 35 cm). The Museum of Modern Art, New York. Gift of Mr. and Mrs. Henry R. Kravis

**MAN RAY
(EMMANUEL RADNITZKY)**
Indestructible Object (or Object to Be Destroyed)
1964 (replica of 1923 original). Metronome with cutout photograph of eye on pendulum, 8 7/8 x 4 3/8 x 4 5/8" (22.5 x 11 x 11.6 cm). The Museum of Modern Art, New York. James Thrall Soby Fund. © 2005 Man Ray Trust/Artists Rights Society (ARS), New York/ADAGP, Paris

PAUL KLEE
Mask of Fear
1932. Oil on burlap, 39 5/8 x 22 1/2" (100.4 x 57.1 cm). The Museum of Modern Art, New York. Nelson A. Rockefeller Fund. © 2005 Artists Rights Society (ARS), New York/VG Bild-Kunst, Bonn

MARCEL DUCHAMP
Bicycle Wheel
1951 (third version, after lost original of 1913). Metal wheel mounted on painted wooden stool, 50 1/2 x 25 1/2 x 16 5/8" (128.3 x 63.8 x 42 cm). The Museum of Modern Art, New York. The Sidney and Harriet Janis Collection. © 2005 Artists Rights Society (ARS), New York/ADAGP, Paris/Estate of Marcel Duchamp

WILLIE COLE
The Artist's Studio
1992. Steam iron scorches and pencil on paper, mounted in dilapidated and recycled painted wooden window frame, composition (including frame): 35 x 32 x 1 3/8" (88.9 x 81.3 x 3.5 cm). The Museum of Modern Art, New York. Acquired through the generosity of Agnes Gund. © 2005 Willie Cole

EUGÈNE ATGET
Saint-Cloud
June 1926. Gelatin silver printing-out-paper print, 6 7/8 x 8 7/8" (17.5 x 22.5 cm). The Museum of Modern Art, New York. Abbott-Levy Collection. Partial gift of Shirley C. Burden.

FRIEDRICH WILHELM MURNAU
Nosferatu
1922. 35mm film, black and white, silent, 88 minutes (approx.). Max Schreck

DOROTHEA LANGE
Migrant Mother, Nipomo, California
1936. Gelatin silver print, 11 1/8 x 8 9/16" (28.3 x 21.8 cm). The Museum of Modern Art, New York. Purchase

NAM JUNE PAIK
Untitled
1993. Player piano, fifteen televisions, two cameras, two laser disc players, one electric light and light bulb, and wires, overall size (including laser disc player and lamp): c. 8' 4" x 8' 9" x 48" (254 x 266.7 x 121.9 cm). The Museum of Modern Art, New York. Bernhill Fund, Gerald S. Elliot Fund, gift of Margot Paul Ernst, and purchase

GEORGES MÉLIÈS
A Trip to the Moon
1902. 35mm film, black and white, silent, 11 minutes (approx.). Bluette Bernon

BUSTER KEATON, CLYDE BRUCKMAN
The General
1926. 35mm film, black and white, silent, 80 minutes (approx.). Buster Keaton

CLAUDE MONET
Reflections of Clouds on the Water-Lily Pond
c. 1920. Oil on canvas, three sections, each 6' 6" x 14' (200 x 425 cm). The Museum of Modern Art, New York. Mrs. Simon Guggenheim Fund

VERNER PANTON
Stacking Side Chair
1959–60. Polyurethane plastic, 32 1/8 x 19 1/4 x 22 5/8" (81.6 x 48.9 x 57.5 cm). Manufacturer: Vitra-Fehlbaum GmbH, Weil-am-Rhein, West Germany (now Germany). The Museum of Modern Art, New York. Gift of Herman Miller AG, Basel, Switzerland

ANDY WARHOL
Campbell's Soup Cans
1962. Synthetic polymer paint on thirty-two canvases. Each canvas 20 x 16" (50.8 x 40.6 cm). The Museum of Modern Art, New York. Gift of Irving Blum, Nelson A. Rockefeller Bequest, gift of Mr. and Mrs. William A. M. Burden, Abby Aldrich Rockefeller Fund, gift of Nina and Gordon Bunshaft in honor of Henry Moore, Lillie P. Bliss Bequest, Philip Johnson Fund, Frances Keech Bequest, gift of Mrs. Bliss Parkinson, and Florence B. Wesley Bequest (all by exchange). © 2005 Andy Warhol Foundation/ARS, NY/TM Licensed by Campbell's Soup Co. All rights reserved

HENRY MOORE
Family Group
1948–49 (cast 1950). Bronze, 59 1/4 x 46 1/2 x 29 7/8" (150.5 x 118 x 75.9 cm). The Museum of Modern Art, New York. A. Conger Goodyear Fund. Reproduced by permission of the Henry Moore Foundation

PABLO PICASSO
She-Goat
1950 (cast 1952). Bronze, 46 3/8 x 56 3/8 x 28 1/8" (117.7 x 143.1 x 71.4 cm). The Museum of Modern Art, New York. Mrs. Simon Guggenheim Fund. © 2005 Estate of Pablo Picasso/Artists Rights Society (ARS), New York

JASPER JOHNS
Map
1961. Oil on canvas, 6' 6" x 10' 3 1/8" (198.2 x 314.7 cm). The Museum of Modern Art, New York. Gift of Mr. and Mrs. Robert C. Scull. © 2005 Jasper Johns/Licensed by VAGA, New York

BARNETT NEWMAN
Broken Obelisk
1963–69. Cor-Ten steel, in two parts, 24' 10" x 10' 11" x 10' 11" (749.9 x 318.8 x 318.8 cm). The Museum of Modern Art, New York. Given anonymously. © 2005 Barnett Newman Foundation/Artists Rights Society (ARS), New York

PAUL KLEE
Cat and Bird
1928. Oil and ink on gessoed canvas, mounted on wood, 15 x 21" (38.1 x 53.2 cm). The Museum of Modern Art, New York. Sidney and Harriet Janis Collection Fund and gift of Suzy Prudden and Joan H. Meijer in memory of F. H. Hirschland. © 2005 Artists Rights Society (ARS), New York/VG Bild-Kunst, Bonn

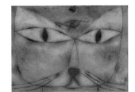

PAUL GAUGUIN
The Seed of the Areoi
1892. Oil on burlap, 36 1/4 x 28 3/8" (92.1 x 72.1 cm). The Museum of Modern Art, New York. The William S. Paley Collection

GEORGE GROSZ
Circe
1927. Watercolor, ink, and pencil on paper, 25 7/8 x 19 1/8" (66 x 48.6 cm). The Museum of Modern Art, New York. Gift of Mr. and Mrs. Walter Bareiss and an anonymous donor (by exchange). © 2005 Artists Rights Society (ARS), New York/VG Bild-Kunst, Bonn

ALDO ROSSI, GIANNI BRAGHIERI
Cemetery of San Cataldo, Modena, Italy
1971. Plan: ink, color ink, and graphite on tracing paper, 23 1/2 x 29 3/4" (59.7 x 75.6 cm). The Museum of Modern Art, New York. Gift of The Howard Gilman Foundation

FRIDA KAHLO
Self-Portrait with Cropped Hair
1940. Oil on canvas, 15 3/4 x 11" (40 x 27.9 cm). The Museum of Modern Art, New York. Gift of Edgar Kaufmann, Jr.

ALVAR AALTO
Paimio Chair
1931–32. Bent plywood, bent laminated birch, and solid birch, 26 x 23 3/4 x 34 1/2" (66 x 60.3 x 87.6 cm). Manufacturer: Oy Huonekalu-ja Rakennustyötehdas Ab, Turku, Finland. The Museum of Modern Art, New York. Gift of Edgar Kaufmann, Jr.

AMEDEO MODIGLIANI
Head
1915? Limestone, 22 1/4 x 5 x 14 3/4" (56.5 x 12.7 x 37.4 cm). The Museum of Modern Art, New York. Gift of Abby Aldrich Rockefeller in memory of Mrs. Cornelius J. Sullivan

JOHN HEARTFIELD (HELMUT HERZFELDE)
Der Sumpf [The Jungle] by Upton Sinclair

Berlin: Malik-Verlag. 1922. Letterpress, 7 3/8 x 17 1/2" (18.7 x 44.5 cm). The Museum of Modern Art, New York. Jan Tschichold Collection, Gift of Philip Johnson. © 2005 Artists Rights Society (ARS), New York/VG Bild-Kunst, Bonn

GUSTAV KLUCIS
Maquette for Radio-Announcer

1922. Construction of painted cardboard, paper, wood, thread, and metal brads, 45 3/4 x 14 1/2 x 14 1/2" (106.1 x 36.8 x 36.8 cm). The Museum of Modern Art, New York. Sidney and Harriet Janis Collection Fund

PABLO PICASSO
Guitar

1913. Pasted paper, charcoal, ink, and chalk on blue paper mounted on ragboard, 26 1/8 x 19 1/2" (66.4 x 49.6 cm). The Museum of Modern Art, New York. Nelson A. Rockefeller Bequest. © 2005 Estate of Pablo Picasso/Artists Rights Society (ARS), New York

FRANK O. GEHRY
Bubbles Chaise Longue

1987. Corrugated cardboard with fire-retardant coating, 27 3/4 x 29 x 76 3/8" (70.5 x 73.7 x 194 cm). Manufacturer: New City Editions, Venice, Calif. The Museum of Modern Art, New York. Kenneth Walker Fund

GEORGE SEGAL
The Bus Driver

1962. Figure: plaster over cheesecloth, with bus parts including coin box, steering wheel, driver's seat, railing, dashboard, etc., figure: 53 1/2 x 26 7/8 x 45" (136 x 68.2 x 114 cm); overall size, 7'5" x 51 5/8" x 6'4 3/4" (226 x 131 x 195 cm). The Museum of Modern Art, New York. Philip Johnson Fund

VLADIMIR MAYAKOVSKY
The Soviet Alphabet by Vladimir Mayakovsky

Page 28. Moscow: the author. 1919. Edition: 3,000-5,000. Book: 30 pages, 7 9/16 x 9 5/8" (19.2 x 24.5 cm) (irreg.). Cover with lithographed manuscript design with watercolor additions on front; lithographed manuscript text incorporating 28 illustrations with watercolor additions. The Museum of Modern Art, New York. Gift of The Judith Rothschild Foundation

MAX ERNST
The Hat Makes the Man

1920. Gouache and pencil on cut-and-pasted printed papers on board with ink inscriptions, 14 x 18" (35.6 x 45.7 cm). The Museum of Modern Art, New York. Purchase. © 2005 Artists Rights Society (ARS), New York/ADAGP, Paris

JEAN ARP (HANS ARP)
Collage with Squares Arranged According to the Laws of Chance

1916–17. Torn and pasted papers on blue-gray paper, 19 1/8 x 13 5/8" (48.5 x 34.6 cm). The Museum of Modern Art, New York. Purchase. © 2005 Artists Rights Society (ARS), New York/VG Bild-Kunst, Bonn

HENRI MATISSE
The Swimming Pool

1952. Nine-panel mural in two parts: gouache on paper, cut and pasted, on white painted paper mounted on burlap, a-e: 7' 6 5/8" x 27' 9 1/2" (230.1 x 847.8 cm); f-i: 7' 6 5/8" x 26' 1 1/2" (230.1 x 796.1 cm). The Museum of Modern Art, New York. Mrs. Bernard F. Gimbel Fund. © 2005 Succession H. Matisse, Paris/Artists Rights Society (ARS), New York

PANAMARENKO
Flying Object (Rocket)

1969. Balsa wood, cardboard, plastic, fabric, aluminum, steel, and synthetic polymer paint, 8' 11" x 11' 4" x 8' 2" (271.7 x 345.5 x 249 cm). The Museum of Modern Art, New York. Gift of Agnes Gund. © 2005 Panamarenko

VLADIMIR LEBEDEV
The Elephant's Child by Rudyard Kipling

Petrograd: Epokha. 1922. Edition: 1,500. Book: 14 pages, 10 1/2 x 8 1/16" (26.7 x 20.7 cm). Cover with letterpress illustration on front; 11 letterpress illustrations. The Museum of Modern Art, New York. Gift of The Judith Rothschild Foundation

JOAN MIRÓ
The Hunter (Catalan Landscape)

1923–1924. Oil on canvas, 25 1/2 x 39 1/2" (64.8 x 100.3 cm). The Museum of Modern Art, New York. Purchase. © 2005 Successió Miró/Artists Rights Society (ARS), New York/ADAGP, Paris

PABLO PICASSO
The Kitchen

1948. Oil on canvas, 69" x 8' 2 1/2" (175.3 x 250 cm). The Museum of Modern Art, New York. Acquired through the Nelson A. Rockefeller Bequest. © 2005 Estate of Pablo Picasso/Artists Rights Society (ARS), New York

ADOLPH GOTTLIEB
Tournament

1951. Oil on canvas, 60 1/8" x 6' 1/8" (152.6 x 183 cm). The Museum of Modern Art, New York. Gift of Esther Gottlieb

ALEXANDER CALDER
Model for Teodelapio

1962. Stabile: painted sheet aluminum, 23 3/4 x 15 1/4 x 15 3/4" (60.3 x 38.7 x 39.8 cm). The Museum of Modern Art, New York. Gift of the artist. © 2005 Estate of Alexander Calder/Artists Rights Society (ARS), New York

GEORGE GROSZ
"The Convict": Monteur John Heartfield after Franz Jung's Attempt to Get Him Up on His Feet

1920. Watercolor, pencil, cut-and-pasted postcards, and halftone relief on paper, 16 1/2 x 12" (41.9 x 30.5 cm). The Museum of Modern Art, New York. Gift of A. Conger Goodyear, 1952